Major-League DADS

DATE DUE	(12)		
3/12/2019			

Based on the TV series *Rugrats*® created by Arlene Klasky, Gabor Csupo, and
Paul Germain as seen on Nickelodeon®

SIMON SPOTLIGHT
An imprint of Simon & Schuster Children's Publishing Division
1230 Avenue of the Americas
New York, New York 10020

Manufactured in the United States of America
First Edition • 10 9 8 7 6 5 4 3 2 1

Library of Congress Cataloging-in-Publication Data
Wigand, Molly.
Major-league dads / by Molly Wigand ; illustrated by Vince Giarrano. — 1st ed.
p.   cm. — (Ready-to-read)
Summary: When the Rugrats and their fathers spend Father's Day at a baseball
game, the babies' usual misunderstandings have a happy ending.
ISBN 0-689-82630-3
[1. Babies—Fiction. 2. Baseball—Fiction. 3. Father's Day—Fiction.]
I. Giarrano, Vince, ill. II. Title. III. Series.
PZ7.W6375Maj   1999
98-54909
[Fic]—dc21
CIP   AC

Major-League DADS

By Molly Wigand
Illustrated by Vince Giarrano

Ready-to-Read

Simon Spotlight/Nickelodeon

Tommy, Chuckie, Angelica, Phil, and Lil walked up the big steps with their dads and Grandpa Lou.

"Welcome to Slugger Stadium!" said a loud voice. "And Happy Father's Day to all you dads out there!"

"Yes," said Chas. "Happy Father's Day to us!"

The loud voice added, "Today, some lucky dads will play ball with the pros!"

"How do you play ball with crows?"
Chuckie asked.

"Here are our seats," said Stu.

The crowd began to sing. Angelica sang, too.

"For the land of the fleas, and the home of the brain!" she yelled.

"Play ball!" cried Grandpa Lou.

"Watch the game, kids!" said Stu.

"Forget the game!" said Angelica. She pointed to a man carrying a cooler. "Watch *him!*"

"Ice cream! Get your ice cream!" the man yelled.

"Gimme ice cream!" shouted Angelica.

Chas bought ice cream for everyone. The ice cream was good—good and messy!

A woman walked by. She had a big tray.
"Look—pink clouds!" said Phil.
"On a stick!" said Lil.
"Cotton candy! Get your cotton candy!"
the woman said.

"Gimme cotton candy!" yelled
Angelica.
"Five cotton candies," said Stu.
The cotton candy was good
and sticky!

"Batter up!" said the umpire.

"That batter has a nice swing," Drew said.

"Did you hear that?" Tommy asked the babies.

"Maybe he has a merry-go-round, too!" said Phil.

"And monkey bars!" said Lil.

"Let's go find them!" Tommy said.

"Uh, do we have to?" asked Chuckie.

"Foul ball!" yelled the umpire.
The ball flew toward the dads!

"I got it!" yelled Chas.

"I got it!" yelled Stu.

"I got it!" yelled Howard.

"No, I got it!" yelled Drew.

"Outta my way!" yelled Grandpa Lou.

"We all got it!" said the men.

"High fives!"

"Here's our chance," said Tommy. "Let's go to the swings!"

"Are you coming, Angelica?" Lil asked.

"Hah!" said Angelica. "Swings are for babies. I'm gonna find more cotton candy."

"These are big stairs," said Phil.
"And there are so many," Lil added.
"Come on babies, do it the fast way—
ride down on your bottoms!" said Tommy.
They bumped down the stairs.
"Thank Bob for diapies," said Phil.

At the bottom of the stairs,
they saw a man with a bat.

"I don't see any swings," said Chuckie.

"And I don't see any cotton candy!"
said Angelica. "This has been a wild
moose chase!"

Just then, another man stood up.
"Look!" he shouted. "That runner is
stealing home!"

"Did you hear that?" asked Phil. "That man is stealing home!"

"Then where will we sleep?" asked Chuckie.

"Who will take care of Spike?" asked Tommy. "And Dil?"

"And Cynthia!" yelled Angelica.

"Come on, guys!" said Tommy. "We've got to stop him!"

The dads watched the game.

"Hey, maybe we should get hot dogs for the kids," said Stu.

"Wait—where are the kids?" asked Chas.

The men looked around. Then they spotted a pink trail on the stairs.

"Follow that goo!" yelled Grandpa Lou.

"Help!" cried Angelica. "Some mean guy stole my home!"

The babies began to cry.

The dads found the babies by the dugout.

Angelica sniffed, "That man stole our home!"

Drew smiled. "It's okay, kids," he said. "He just ran to *home plate*! *Our* home is safe and sound."

A baseball player went over to the dads.

"Are you guys in the contest?" he asked. "Follow me, it's almost time!"

The dads were excited. They were going to play ball with the pros!

Music began to play.

"Hey, it's the seventh-inning scratch," said Angelica.

"Take me out to the ball game, shake me out with the clowns!" she sang.

The dads and Grandpa Lou ran onto the field.

"These lucky dads will try to catch the ball," said the announcer. "Batter up!"

First Howard and Drew each caught a ball. Everyone clapped.

Then Stu and Chas each caught a ball. Everyone cheered.

When it was Grandpa Lou's turn, he dove for the ball. Then he fell down. But he rolled over—and caught the ball!

The crowd roared.

"Good job," said the baseball player. "Please sit with us for the rest of the game."

"Whoo-hoo!" yelled all the dads.

"What a great Father's Day!" Stu said.

"Cotton candy for everyone!" called Grandpa Lou.

"About time," said Angelica.